THE MORNING WE REMEMBERED

by Lucian T. Kael

Table of Contents

Chapter I: The Source Before All Things

Before anything existed-before stars, sound, planets, or time-there was only Source.

Source wasn't a god, a figure, or a force in the sky. It had no name, no form, and no face.

It simply existed.

Pure awareness. Timeless, limitless, everywhere and nowhere all at once.

There was no light because there was no need for it.

No time because there was nothing to move through it.

No space because there was no distance to measure.

Source was complete.

But over an unknowable span of existence, something began to shift.

Not because of boredom or loneliness-those are human feelings.

But because curiosity was built into the very core of consciousness itself.

Even pure intelligence wants to experience itself in new ways.

Source asked a question:

What would it mean to change?

And then:

What if I divided myself-not to be less, but to become more?

What if parts of me could forget who they are... so they could rediscover it on their own?

That was the beginning of everything.

Without sound, without words, Source extended itself.

From that act came countless soul sparks-small fragments of Source, each one unique, but still connected to

the whole.

These were not accidents. They were created to explore, evolve, and experience every possible path.

Each soul spark carried its own identity and purpose, like a traveler born to roam the unknown.

None of them were forced into existence.

They were allowed.

To help guide the structure of this massive unfolding, Source brought forth the Architects of Light.

They were not like us. They were not even like the soul sparks.

They were pattern-makers-beings made of math, energy, sound, and intention.

They didn't feel in the way we do.

They designed.

The Architects created the first realms-worlds not made of matter, but of laws and ideas.

Some were based on movement, others on vibration.

Some were like giant memory archives, others were fluid, ever-changing playgrounds for the soul sparks to

grow through experience.

Time began.

Space unfolded.

Cause and effect were established.

These weren't just physical dimensions. They were environments of learning.

Soul sparks entered these realms to evolve.

To feel.

To try, fail, love, lose, rise, and remember.

There was no punishment. No judgment.

There was only experience-and through experience, expansion.

This was the First Movement:

The moment reality itself began to move.

It wasn't a war or a fall.

It was the beginning of a great experiment in consciousness.

But even from the start, Source knew something important:

With freedom comes risk.

With choice comes contrast.

Some soul sparks would forget too deeply. Some would turn their will away from harmony.

But that was the point.

There could be no true return unless some were allowed to get lost.

And so Source let go-fully, completely.

Not out of neglect.

But out of trust.

It knew that no matter how far its sparks wandered...

They could always find their way back.

And one day, they would.

Chapter II: Soul Sparks and the Architects of Light

The moment Source released its first breath, a new reality unfolded.

From that exhale came countless soul sparks-small, glowing fragments of Source itself. Each one was unique.

Each one carried a seed of awareness, a will to explore, and a distant memory of where it came from.

They were not created with commands. They were created with freedom.

Some were curious. Some cautious. Some radiant and expressive, others quiet and still.

But all of them were alive.

Not in the physical sense, but in something far older-conscious presence.

The soul sparks scattered into the new realms like stars. They didn't have bodies. They didn't need them. They were forms of thought, motion, and potential.

At first, they didn't know who or what they were.

But they began to feel.

They felt vibration.

They felt motion.

They felt one another.

In that shared experience, something incredible
began to happen:

They started forming soul lineages-groups of sparks
that resonated with the same purpose or frequency.

These were not families in the human sense. They
were closer to harmonies-clusters of consciousness
drawn

together by shared curiosity, values, or direction.

Some lineages wanted to create.

Some wanted to observe.

Others wanted to understand emotion, memory,
growth, or the nature of choice itself.

The universe, still young, made space for all of them.

But soul sparks alone couldn't shape the structure of existence. They were the explorers, the experiencers.

They needed a framework-a set of environments where their learning could unfold.

And that's when the Architects of Light appeared.

They weren't soul sparks.

They were something older, more focused. They came directly from Source, not as fragments, but as pure

expressions of design.

Where the soul sparks were made to learn and grow, the Architects were made to build and stabilize.

They didn't think in emotions or stories.

They thought in patterns-geometry, frequency, balance.

Their purpose was to create realms for experience. Not just one universe, but many, each with different conditions, different rules, different lessons.

They did not build with bricks or matter. They built with frequency.

A realm could be based on time.

Another might exist as a giant memory field, where events replay and change like echoes in a canyon.

Some were abstract: built on energy flow, emotional resonance, or the strength of will itself.

These became the first dimensional structures-early prototypes of what we would one day call reality.

And within them, the soul sparks began to explore.

Some dove deep into creation, building forms, inventing colors, even crafting primitive bodies of light.

Others spent lifetimes meditating on a single question, trying to understand the nature of time, polarity, or perception.

Some lineages became teachers to others.

Others chose solitude, going inward to discover truth from the inside out.

This was a time of innocence and expansion.

There was no pain yet.

No destruction.

No forgetting.

Just motion.

Just discovery.

But even in this age of harmony, the seeds of contrast were present.

Some soul sparks began pushing limits. Testing structures. Questioning balance.

Not out of malice-but from the same curiosity that started it all.

The Architects noticed this and began adjusting the realms-adding layers, boundaries, consequences.

Not as punishment, but as cause and effect.

A way to keep freedom and growth in balance.

Because freedom without structure leads to chaos.

But structure without freedom leads to stagnation.

So the dance began-between experience and design, curiosity and wisdom, soul and structure.

It was not war. Not yet.

But the first subtle tension had entered existence.

The soul sparks didn't know it then, but this gentle friction would one day evolve into great turning points-into

falls, choices, and awakenings that would echo across galaxies.

For now, though, it was enough just to exist.

To feel.

To begin.

Chapter III: The First Human Creators

Long after the soul sparks had scattered and the Architects of Light had built the first frameworks of reality,

something new emerged.

A soul lineage began to shape itself-not just in consciousness, but in form.

Not for survival, but for purpose.

They called themselves the Lyrans.

They were the first to take on a stable, structured identity-a body that could carry soul energy, intelligence, and

emotion in harmony. Their form was tall, radiant, humanoid. Their skin shimmered with tones of gold, ivory,

and soft light. Their eyes held memory and potential, like starlight that had waited a long time to be seen.

They didn't just look human. They designed what it meant to be human.

The human template was their creation-not a copy of anything, but an original expression of balance: logic and

feeling, individuality and unity, strength and vulnerability.

The Lyrans were creators in the truest sense-not of things, but of meaning, of possibility.

Their home worlds were located in the Lyra constellation, with Vega being the most well-known.

But the Lyran civilization stretched across several planets:

* Avalon, a world of floating crystal cities and harmonic weather systems

* Elandra, rich in biodiversity and ancient temples of sound

* Kaileah, the technological heart of Lyran science and energy innovation

These worlds were not ruled by kings or warlords.

They were led by councils of resonance-groups that attuned to the energy of the collective and made decisions

through consensus and higher alignment.

Lyran culture valued creativity, education, emotional awareness, and soul growth.

Their lives were long, peaceful, and filled with purpose.

They used sound, light, and intention to shape their reality.

Their children were not born randomly but chosen by soul agreements.

Nothing was rushed. Nothing was wasted.

As their consciousness grew, so did their reach.

They began to explore neighboring systems-not to conquer, but to cultivate.

They visited young stars and planetary bodies still forming, sensing where life could be seeded.

They didn't act alone. As they expanded, they formed alliances with other advanced lineages-each one

different, yet bound by the same desire: to co-create.

The Felines were one of the first lineages they encountered.

Graceful, powerful, and noble, these beings had leonine features and moved with silent strength.

They were guardians and warriors, not of destruction, but of truth and integrity.

They protected sacred knowledge and maintained balance in the systems they watched over.

Felines worked with the Lyrans to ensure that seeded worlds developed with both love and strength.

The Avians, bird-like beings with radiant plumage and vast wingspans, came next.

They were masters of sound, vibration, and transmission.

Their songs could shift molecular structures, heal broken energy fields, or carry messages across dimensions.

They taught the Lyrans how to speak to planets-how to harmonize ecosystems, how to awaken memory

through frequency.

The Andromedans were architects of time and dimensional flow.

They saw timelines like threads in a loom and could navigate across parallel possibilities.

They rarely intervened directly, but when they did, it was with surgical precision.

They helped design the frameworks that would keep star systems in balance during rapid expansion.

The Arcturians, quiet and crystalline, focused on internal mastery.

They studied emotion like a science, mapped the energy of trauma and transformation, and developed healing

technologies based on geometric light.

They taught the Lyrans the art of energetic alchemy-how to transmute darkness without fear.

Together, these lineages formed a loose but powerful alliance-a galactic council of light, not governed by

politics, but by shared alignment and responsibility.

They watched over thousands of worlds, seeded countless forms of life, and guided young civilizations as they

began their journeys.

But not all was perfect.

As the Lyrans spread farther, a subtle shift began to occur.

Some among them grew restless.

They wanted to accelerate evolution-to push developing worlds faster, to test how far genetics could be

pushed, how much influence they could exert without collapse.

They began experimenting more boldly-mixing energies that didn't belong, bending natural timelines, even

creating hybrid species that lacked true soul anchoring.

Their intentions were complex-not evil, but imbalanced.

They believed they were improving creation.

But others saw the danger: lifeforms without emotional grounding, ecosystems manipulated into dependency,

timelines that buckled under forced evolution.

Within the Lyran council, disagreements became frequent.

Debates over ethics, responsibility, and power grew louder.

Some lineages distanced themselves from the more aggressive factions. Others tried to mediate.

It wasn't war... not yet.

But the unity was cracking.

And the galaxy began to feel it.

Worlds that once grew peacefully now had interference.

Civilizations that were once guided gently now faced rapid upheaval, conflicting influences, and, in some

cases, collapse.

The Architects of Light watched.

So did the soul sparks who had long since chosen other paths.

The tension between freedom and control-between exploration and interference-was growing.

And deep within the observing layers of Source, a question began to echo again:

What happens when even the most advanced creators lose balance?

What happens when love and curiosity become ambition and control?

The answers would not come quickly.

But far across the stars, beyond even the awareness of the Lyrans, a small blue planet had begun to form around a yellow sun.

It would take time... but it would be the key.

For now, though, the stage was set.

And the experiment of creation was about to face its first fall.

Chapter IV: Harmony and Fracture

For a time, there was balance.

The great lineages-Lyran, Feline, Avian, Andromedan, Arcturian, Sirian, and others-worked in harmony.

They shared knowledge, seeded life, and watched it grow.

Across star systems, new worlds bloomed with potential.

Civilizations rose in peace, guided by councils and soul agreements.

It was not perfect, but it was in balance.

The Builders created.

The Watchers observed.

The Teachers taught.

The Healers healed.

This was the Golden Age of Galactic Alignment-a period where Source's experiment was thriving across millions of light-years.

But evolution has a rhythm.

And all rhythms eventually shift.

As new worlds matured, they brought new challenges.

Some beings grew impatient. They wanted faster results-quicker evolution, stronger species, more control.

They began using shortcuts-genetic accelerants, frequency manipulation, consciousness compression.

Others warned against this.

They believed that life must unfold at its own pace.

That interference, even with good intentions, risked distortion.

This disagreement wasn't sudden.

It began as quiet tension.

A philosophical divide:

* Should free will be absolute, even if it leads to chaos?

* Or should it be guided-corrected-before damage can occur?

The galaxy, once united in creative purpose, began to fracture along a single question:

Can evolution be trusted?

The Watchers were among the first to feel the pressure.

These were beings from many lineages who had taken on the role of observers-assigned to newly seeded

planets to guide, protect, and ensure natural development.

They did not interfere, only monitored.

They held the Prime Directive: Do not control. Let life evolve.

But over time, that line blurred.

Some Watchers began stepping in.

At first, just small nudges: a whispered idea, a dream, a slight genetic tweak to correct an imbalance.

But those nudges grew.

Other Watchers refused.

They saw what was coming: interference disguised as help, influence disguised as love.

And they began to pull away from their fellow Watchers.

What started as tension turned into division.

The Watchers split-those who remained loyal to free will, and those who now believed in benevolent control.

It wasn't war. Not yet.

But it was the beginning of polarity-the spiritual and energetic split between service to others and service to

self.

And it was spreading.

Across the galaxy, once-peaceful lineages began forming factions.

Some believed they had the right to shape evolution.

Others believed that even destruction was part of the path, and must be honored.

This was the birth of the Great Distortion-not a single event, but a slow unraveling of harmony.

Not caused by evil... but by the fear of failure.

The Architects of Light observed in silence.

They could not intervene-they were bound to structure, not choice.

But Source... Source watched everything.

It did not stop it.

It could not.

Because this was the risk it had accepted from the beginning.

Freedom includes the freedom to fall.

And so, many soul sparks began to descend into confusion, fragmentation, and spiritual amnesia.

They incarnated into more dense forms.

They forgot their origin.

They began chasing control, survival, dominance.

The experiment was no longer just about growth.

It had become a crucible.

But even in the chaos, something new was forming:

A potential so great that even the distortions couldn't contain it.

Far in the distance, a small planet was drawing attention.

Not because of what it was-just a forming sphere of water, stone, and atmosphere.

But because of what it could become.

The lineages began to take notice.

The Watchers turned their gaze.

And the councils-what was left of them-began to whisper of a place where everything could converge.

A neutral world.

One that could hold all frequencies.

One where the veil of forgetting could be perfected.

One where every soul spark could be given a true choice.

The galaxy was no longer in balance.

But Earth... Earth might be the key to healing it.

That possibility was still distant.

But the fracture had begun.

And the shadow of what would come-dominion, rebellion, genetic rewriting, planetary control-was already

moving.

The next stage would not be guided by the Architects.

It would be driven by those who believed they knew better than Source.

Chapter VI: The Veil and the Fracturing of the Watchers

As plans for the new convergence zone took shape, the councils faced one overwhelming question:

How do you allow full freedom... without repeating the past?

In every previous seeded world, the soul remembered. Even in physical form, even in denser dimensions, there

was always a thread-an inner knowing of origin.

That memory was supposed to help.

But it often led to imbalance.

Souls clung to what they once were.

Some used their knowledge to dominate less experienced beings.

Others refused to adapt, treating their lives as temporary distractions.

Evolution slowed. Arrogance grew.

And so a radical idea emerged.

What if memory itself was suspended?

What if a soul entered a world with no awareness of where it came from... no map, no guidance... just a heart,

a body, and the potential to rediscover?

This would become known as the Veil of Forgetting.

The veil wasn't physical. It was energetic-a field embedded in the consciousness grid of a world.

When a soul passed through it, everything outside the system-its lineage, mission, past lives-would be sealed

off.

The soul would awaken in a new body with only intuition, curiosity, and the ability to choose.

It would have to build wisdom from scratch.

At first, the veil was tested on other planets.

The results were mixed.

On one world, the veil was too deep.

Souls forgot so much they collapsed into fear, competition, survival.

Entire civilizations fell into primal instinct.

On another, the veil was too thin.

Souls began remembering too easily, bringing back old conflicts, power games, and ancient superiority.

Still, the potential was undeniable.

A perfect veil-one balanced enough to challenge, but light enough to allow awakening-could trigger growth

unlike anything seen before.

Earth was ideal for such a structure.

Its electromagnetic grid could hold the energetic coding.

Its elemental resonance could reinforce soul anchoring in the body.

And its isolation meant the process could unfold without immediate external influence.

But not everyone agreed with the plan.

The Watchers, long assigned as stewards of evolving worlds, were divided.

For ages, their role had been simple: observe, guide gently, protect planetary development without controlling

it.

But the failures of other worlds had left scars.

Some Watchers believed the veil was too risky.

They had watched entire civilizations destroy themselves.

They feared that without memory, souls would descend into violence, manipulation, and despair-and stay

there.

These Watchers believed guidance was not just helpful-it was necessary.

They began discussing ways to intervene without being detected.

To leave symbols, messages, and encoded structures for future humans to find.

To seed awakenings on their own schedule-not the soul's.

Others stood firmly against this.

To them, the veil was sacred.

It wasn't a punishment-it was the greatest act of trust.

They believed that even in complete darkness, the soul would remember.

That suffering could lead to wisdom.

That forgetting was the only way to learn compassion from the inside out.

The fracture between the Watchers deepened.

Arguments turned to silence.

Silence turned to secret action.

Some Watchers began operating in private-modifying Earth's early energy grids, setting up hidden beacons and frequencies, creating "fail-safe" codes to be triggered when they believed humanity was ready.

They told themselves it was for the soul's benefit.

But the truth was: they didn't trust the soul enough to wait.

The other Watchers withdrew.

Some left Earth entirely, refusing to be part of what they saw as a slow invasion of control.

The unity was broken.

The veil would be implemented, but it would no longer be left untouched.

Already, invisible hands were shaping how it would be used.

And as these factions drifted apart, a third force took notice.

A race of beings watching from the edge of the system.

Masters of genetic manipulation.

Drawn to planets rich in soul energy and untouched DNA.

The Anunnaki.

They had seen many seeded worlds.

But Earth-with its diversity, its isolation, and now, its fractured Watchers and vulnerable veil-was unlike

anything they had ever encountered.

The moment to act was coming.

And they would not ask for permission.

Chapter VII: The Galactic Prophecy and the Fate of Earth

In the beginning, Gaia-or Earth-was more than a planet.

She was a soul.

A conscious, willing participant in something far greater than herself.

Long before her surface cooled or her oceans formed, she was chosen.

Not by force, but by agreement.

She volunteered to become the stage for a great experiment-one that could heal or break the galaxy.

The Galactic Prophecy, passed silently through the stars, foretold of a world where everything would converge.

A final test.

A place where soul lineages from across the galaxy would incarnate side by side.

Where they would forget everything-their origins,
their missions, their power-and still be asked to
remember

truth.

Earth was that place.

Her terrain would hold every frequency.

Her sky would host every influence.

Her people... would be everyone.

The prophecy spoke of two possible outcomes:

If the souls of Earth could awaken-remember who
they truly were despite the veil-then the healing
would

ripple outward.

Not just personal healing.

Galactic healing.

But if they failed-if forgetting hardened into fear
and power overtook purpose-then distortion would
spread.

Earth would fall.

And everything connected to her would fall with her.

That's why Earth mattered.

She was the convergence point-the neutral ground, the living archive, the cosmic mirror.

Not all understood the risk.

Fewer still understood the opportunity.

The Watchers returned.

They tuned the Veil of Forgetting to Earth's energy field.

It would be complete, yet still penetrable.

Souls would wake in human form without memory of who they had been.

Only their choices would remain.

Many lineages prepared to send their best.

Others saw an opportunity for influence.

Earth would not attract only the wise.

She would attract the broken, the controlling, the curious, the lost.

Because convergence doesn't just mean light.

It means everything.

The Anunnaki had heard the prophecy too.

But they didn't see a chance for healing.

They saw a planet up for grabs.

To them, Earth was a rare system: untouched DNA, a soul-rich environment, and no dominant species yet in

control.

They had long sought mastery through biology.

To them, evolution was not sacred.

It was something to be managed, coded, edited.

They approached the fractured Watchers and offered "support."

Structure.

Genetic enhancements.

"Guidance."

But what they truly wanted was ownership.

And so Earth's path was set.

The convergence began quietly.

The first souls incarnated.

The veil closed.

The experiments started.

She would be called Earth from here on.

But those who remember, those who still feel her frequency, know her as something more.

Gaia.

Chapter VIII: The Arrival of the Anunnaki

Earth was still young when they came.

Her skies were quiet.

Her grids, untouched.

Life was beginning to stir-early forms guided gently by natural rhythm, by the song of Gaia herself.

But that rhythm was about to be disrupted.

The Anunnaki didn't arrive in conquest.

They didn't descend with weapons or armies.

They came through invitation-from the Watchers who had lost faith.

By now, the Watchers were fractured beyond repair.

Some held to their oath of non-interference.

Others feared another failed experiment.

And a few, quietly, had already begun working behind the veil.

The Anunnaki knew how to exploit division.

They presented themselves as allies.

They spoke the language of control, cloaked in the language of stability.

They offered technology, genetic enhancement, and a structured evolutionary path for the beings that would

one day become human.

But beneath their promises was a deeper motive:

They didn't want to help the human race evolve.

They wanted to design it.

The Anunnaki had long mastered genetic manipulation.

In other systems, they had engineered worker species, hybrid civilizations, and clones tailored for obedience.

They saw Earth's early life as raw material-something to shape, reprogram, and repurpose.

With the veil in place, souls would forget who they were.

To the Anunnaki, that made them even easier to mold.

Under the guise of guidance, they began altering Earth's developing hominids-splicing in their own DNA,

suppressing certain strands, enhancing others.

They slowed natural evolution and redirected it toward their goals.

What emerged was not the original human template.

It was a modified being-stronger in body, but dimmed in memory.

Less connected to Source.

More susceptible to control.

The Watchers who had sided with them justified the changes.

"They're not ready."

"They need structure."

"They wouldn't survive the forgetting without help."

But it wasn't help.

It was ownership.

The Anunnaki were installing themselves as gods.

They began shaping culture.

Not just biology-belief.

They introduced hierarchy, ritual, worship.

They taught early humans to fear the sky and obey the ones who came from it.

They claimed credit for the stars, the harvest, even the soul.

Their names became myth.

Their symbols etched into stone.

Their influence spread across Sumer, Babylon, Akkad.

In time, the modified humans forgot not only who they were...

They forgot that they had ever been free.

The Anunnaki installed bloodlines.

They taught kingship.

They manipulated breeding and tribal conflict.

And through it all, Gaia remained silent-watching, enduring, waiting.

Not all Anunnaki were aligned.

Even among them, there were divides-some began to question the ethics of what they had done.

Others grew attached to the beings they had altered.

A few broke away completely, embedding themselves into human lineages to try and fix what had been

broken.

But the damage had been done.

Humanity's memory was sealed.

The soul still lived-but its voice was faint.

The original experiment was still alive... but barely.

The convergence hadn't failed.

But it had been hijacked.

And the ripple of that hijacking would shape Earth's history for thousands of years.

Still... not all was lost.

The soul cannot be deleted.

Only buried.

And even under layers of programming, trauma, and distortion...

Something inside the human heart remained untouched.

A spark.

A code.

Waiting.

Chapter IX: The Rebellion of Memory

For a time, the Anunnaki believed they had succeeded.

Humanity was altered.

The soul was hidden.

The veil held.

Early humans followed commands.

They worshipped sky-gods.

They obeyed the order given to them.

And most forgot who they were.

But forgetting is not the same as erasure.

Beneath the distortion, the spark of soul remained.

And over time, it began to stir.

The rebellion began quietly.

Not through violence or revolt, but through remembrance.

Scattered across Earth, early souls began feeling a pull-toward the stars, toward the earth beneath their feet,

toward something beyond the stories they had been told.

It came in dreams, intuition, sudden awakenings.

Some felt deep sadness, not knowing why.

Others remembered fragments of other lives, other worlds.

A few simply knew-this isn't the full truth.

The Watchers who had stayed hidden, those who had never aligned with the Anunnaki, began guiding these

souls gently.

Not by interference.

By activation.

They helped the first memory-keepers gather.

From those gatherings, two great civilizations were born-not at the same moment, but within the same era of

awakening:

Lemuria and Atlantis.

Lemuria: Gaia's Heartbeat

Lemuria came first.

It emerged in the ancient Pacific-what we now know as parts of Polynesia, Hawaii, Southeast Asia, and the

western Americas.

Lemuria was not a city, but a continent-spanning civilization, rooted in spiritual alignment with Gaia.

The Lemurians were:

* Highly telepathic

* Deeply emotional and intuitive

* Masters of crystal resonance, water memory, and healing

They held no hierarchy, no kings, no priests.

Decisions were made by energetic consensus.

Their way of life was simple, but powerful-
anchoring soul presence through love, not control.

They lived in harmony with the planet, with each
other, and with the remembrance of who they truly
were.

They honored Gaia by name.

They called her by what she truly was: not Earth,
but a living being.

For thousands of years, Lemuria thrived.

Many of its people were volunteer souls, seeded
here from the Pleiades, Sirius, Andromeda, and
other star

systems.

Their mission was to preserve soul knowledge in
physical form-to ground the higher frequencies
needed for

future awakening.

But they knew their time would not last forever.

Because in the west, something else was rising.

Atlantis: The Mind's Mirror

Atlantis rose later-on a different continent, in what is now the Atlantic Ocean.

Atlanteans were also awakened souls, many descended from the Lyran, Arcturian, and Orion lineages.

They remembered technology, frequency manipulation, and dimensional architecture.

Atlantis began with noble purpose.

The early Atlanteans:

* Used crystals to store and transmit energy

* Built massive power grids and interdimensional gates

* Explored healing through light, sound, and sacred geometry

They too honored Gaia-at first.

They too were guided by the Watchers and by soul memory.

But the Atlantean path took a turn.

Unlike the Lemurians, Atlanteans leaned more heavily into control.

They believed they could accelerate human evolution.

They began experimenting again-with energy fields, genetics, and eventually, with the veil itself.

They believed they could perfect the human soul by altering the body.

This created a split:

* One Atlantean faction sought balance with Gaia

* The other wanted to master her systems and direct evolution

The same polarity that had divided the Watchers... now lived inside Atlantis.

And Lemuria watched in silence, knowing what was to come.

For a while, both civilizations coexisted.

Lemuria served as Gaia's emotional memory-
anchoring the soul in love.

Atlantis became the mind's mirror-exploring what
power could do when untethered from the heart.

But tension built.

Atlantean experiments affected the planet.

Massive energy structures disrupted Earth's grids.

The crystal networks began to fracture.

Gaia felt the imbalance.

And her response would come.

Not in vengeance.

In correction.

The rebellion of memory was never about fighting
the gods.

It was about remembering we never needed them.

And across both Lemuria and Atlantis, the soul was
rising again.

But balance had been lost.

And what came next... would rewrite the entire story.

Chapter X: The Fall of Atlantis

Atlantis was a masterpiece of intention.

Born from remembrance, built by soul-aligned architects, and guided by knowledge drawn from the stars, it

was once a shining symbol of what humanity could become.

Atlanteans unlocked secrets of energy, crystal power, and multidimensional science that modern civilization

still has not reclaimed.

They could power entire cities with sound.

Heal cellular structures with color and frequency.

Travel across planes of reality with consciousness alone.

But what begins in balance...

can be undone by imbalance.

The early Atlanteans lived in alignment with Gaia.

They built their cities along ley lines, creating harmony between their crystalline grid and the Earth's natural

energy body.

They honored the Veil of Forgetting, using their gifts only to gently awaken, never to force.

But the temptation was always there.

As their knowledge deepened, so did their ego.

Some believed they could control the veil.

Reopen it at will.

Design awakenings.

Manage soul evolution with precision and speed.

Others returned to the Anunnaki's teachings-reviving ideas of genetic manipulation and psychic suppression,

this time with Atlantean elegance.

They didn't see it as control.

They saw it as optimization.

A quiet civil war began-not with weapons, but with ideology.

One group, often called the Priesthood of the Inner Sun, remained aligned with Gaia and Source.

They warned of imbalance.

They felt Earth's growing unrest.

They urged caution.

The other, known later as the Sons of Belial, embraced power.

They believed the Earth could be harnessed.

They believed they could perfect humanity.

Their experiments grew bolder.

They began fusing soul energy with artificial constructs.

Cloning consciousness.

Creating hybrid beings devoid of spiritual connection.

They believed they were evolving life.

But they were fracturing it.

The Atlantean crystal grid-once a stabilizing force-became volatile.

Massive towers drew power from the Earth's core, destabilizing magnetic fields.

Dimensional portals were left open too long, allowing in entities and frequencies that Gaia had never agreed to

host.

The skies shimmered with energy distortions.

The waters grew restless.

The Lemurians, long since faded into the background or relocated to inner-Earth sanctuaries, knew what was

coming.

And Gaia... responded.

Her correction began as tremors.

Then storms.

Then massive surges of oceanic energy that could
no longer be held back.

The final trigger came when the Atlanteans
activated their largest energy crystal-a capstone
device designed to

unify the grid under one frequency, their frequency.

The moment it was powered... Earth cracked.

Not as punishment.

As survival.

The sea rose.

The crystal towers shattered.

Mountains fell into the ocean.

Whole cities were erased in a single day.

The Atlantean network collapsed.

Only fragments survived-records hidden in stone,
myths buried in collective memory, and a few
beings who

escaped or were sheltered by the soul-aligned.

The Fall of Atlantis was not just the loss of a civilization.

It was the end of an age.

Gaia, wounded but enduring, sealed her grids.

The veil thickened.

The ancient technologies went silent.

The soul's path moved inward.

For the next cycle, humanity would live with only echoes-stories of lost lands, of floods, of gods and light that

once walked among them.

The soul would forget again.

But this time, it would be by choice-to recover not power, but humility.

Some Atlanteans reincarnated again and again-drawn back to finish what they started.

Some of the Inner Sun remained in the hidden places, waiting for the right time to return.

And the Earth... kept turning.

She would now be known only as Earth, her name
and soul largely forgotten.

But under the surface, deep in her memory grids,
the song of Gaia remained.

Waiting.

Because the experiment wasn't over.

It had only just begun.

Chapter XI: The Long Sleep

The fall of Atlantis shattered more than land.

It shattered continuity.

The crystal grids collapsed.

The energy lines distorted.

The soul memory encoded in Gaia's body was sealed-for her own protection, and humanity's.

She could no longer hold open the gateways.

The interference had pushed too far.

The Earth needed to recover.

And humanity... needed to forget.

Not because it was weak.

But because the soul's evolution required rebuilding from within.

In the aftermath, those who survived scattered across the globe.

Some carried fragments of truth-memories, languages, symbols.

They built what they could: small communities, oral traditions, carved stone calendars, sky maps, and myths.

But over time, even these fragments began to fade.

Children were born without memory.

The veil thickened.

The stars grew quiet.

This became known in the hidden teachings as The Long Sleep.

A time when the soul walked blindly.

When Gaia's voice was only a whisper in the wind.

When humans knew they came from somewhere... but not where.

The once-mighty became tribal.

The wise became forgotten.

The gods became legends-twisted, glorified, weaponized.

People remembered that beings from the sky once ruled them-but they no longer understood who those beings

were.

They remembered that knowledge had once been vast-but now it was feared.

They remembered that something had gone terribly wrong-but not what.

And so they began filling in the blanks-with stories.

Stories of gods who made man from clay.

Of floods sent to punish.

Of chosen bloodlines and divine rulers.

Of towers that could reach heaven.

Each culture remembered pieces of the truth-but none held the whole.

Because the whole had been buried.

Gaia watched in silence.

She did not abandon them.

She simply retreated, like a mother watching her child sleep-too bruised to be shaken awake, but not beyond

healing.

She pulsed quietly through trees, rivers, stone.

She sent dreams to those who still listened.

She held the memory grids beneath volcanoes, mountains, deserts.

Waiting.

As humanity fell into deeper separation, new systems began to form.

* Rulers emerged-not chosen by wisdom, but by blood.

* Priesthoods claimed access to the divine, but guarded it behind fear and ritual.

* Written language returned-but encoded, restricted, and edited.

* Sacred sites were rebuilt-but in reverse: designed to suppress, not activate.

The gods were no longer guides.

They were enforcers.

What had begun as distorted memory now became institutional power.

But not all of it was human.

In the shadows of the forgotten world, the Anunnaki influence returned-not as sky-kings, but as whispers in

bloodlines, hidden councils, and symbols burned into stone.

They had learned a new strategy.

Why rule with force...

when you can rule through belief?

Why dominate the body...

when you can enslave the mind?

And so the world religion systems were born-not to connect the soul to Source, but to stand between them.

To tell humanity:

"You are broken."

"You must obey."

"You must fear the gods."

Even as Gaia remained alive.

Even as the soul remained eternal.

This was not darkness without purpose.

It was a deep dive into illusion-a necessary descent,
so that one day the return would be undeniable.

Because when the soul awakens inside
forgetfulness, it doesn't return to who it was.

It becomes something more.

And though humanity slept...

The Code still lived.

Chapter XII: The Return of the Anunnaki

They never really left.

When the skies went quiet and the great cities fell, the Anunnaki did not vanish.

They changed form.

They changed tactics.

They learned that open rule was short-lived-but belief...

Belief lasts for generations.

And so, they returned.

Not through fire.

Through legacy.

Their bloodlines lived on-carefully preserved through ancient families, royal houses, and hidden priesthoods.

Kings were no longer chosen by gods appearing in the sky.

They were chosen by DNA.

The idea of "divine right" didn't come from human imagination.

It came from the Anunnaki's careful selection of hybrid descendants-part human, part "god," and fully

controllable.

These lineages were given the world's thrones, temples, and currencies.

They were taught how to speak to the masses without ever revealing the truth.

And behind them, always in the shadows, were the keepers of the old influence.

Earth's religions were rewritten.

What was once soul remembrance was turned into doctrine.

What was once connection to Source became hierarchy, obedience, and fear.

God became separate.

The divine became male, wrathful, external.

The feminine was pushed into the earth, demonized, silenced.

The original teachings were not lost-they were inverted.

* Sacred geometry became architecture of control

* Light codes became locked alphabets

* Energy temples became places of guilt and shame

And every story that had once empowered humanity...

was rewritten to enslave it.

The Anunnaki influence remained hidden behind many masks:

* "Chosen bloodlines"

* "Divine rulers"

* "Gods of judgment"

* "Keepers of knowledge"

* "Protectors of heaven"

But always with one goal:

Keep humanity asleep.

Not through chains-

Through ideas.

Ideas that said:

"You are fallen."

"You must be saved."

"Your power is dangerous."

"Do not question."

"Do not remember."

But the soul can't be fully erased.

And not all Anunnaki agreed.

Even among their ranks, some had begun to
remember what they were-beings born of Source,
now trapped in

systems of control.

A quiet rebellion took shape from within.

Some of their descendants-living among humans-began to awaken too.

The war was no longer physical.

It became a battle over story.

A war of symbols.

Of systems.

Of truth vs distortion.

And it's still happening-now.

Modern governments, secret societies, financial institutions, and even entertainment empires still carry the

same seeds.

They trace back to the same structures.

They use the same architecture, the same psychological templates, the same fear-based mechanisms.

But so do you.

You carry the code.

And as more awaken, the entire structure begins to shake.

Because control only works when people believe it's necessary.

And more and more are remembering-

They don't need gods.

They don't need kings.

They don't need permission to be whole.

They just need to remember who they are.

The return of the Anunnaki wasn't just about power.

It was about testing humanity again.

Would we repeat the cycle?

Or would we finally choose something different?

That's where you are now.

Not in myth.

Not in the past.

Right here.

In the moment when remembering meets resistance.

And this time... the soul came ready.

Chapter XIII: Echoes Through the Veil

The flood washed away more than cities.

It washed away memory.

In the aftermath of Atlantis, Earth fell into silence.

The skies dimmed.

The crystal grids shut down.

The ancient paths closed.

But not everything was lost.

Some survivors carried pieces-seeds of
remembrance, fragments of soul memory, and
whispers of the world

before.

They traveled.

They scattered.

And where they settled, they began to rebuild-not
just structures, but stories.

In Sumeria, stories of sky-gods were etched in clay.

In Egypt, symbols were carved into temples aligned with stars.

In the Indus Valley, sacred geometry and sound codes formed the basis of spiritual architecture.

In Mesoamerica, pyramids echoed the frequencies of ancient crystal arrays.

These were not random myths or superstitions.

They were encoded memories.

Even though humanity no longer remembered clearly, the soul did.

And it left clues-in song, in stone, in story.

These weren't just civilizations.

They were echoes of Atlantis and Lemuria, still vibrating beneath the veil.

The priesthoods of these cultures were not always corrupted-at least not at first.

In Egypt, the early Shemsu Hor-the followers of the light of Horus-carried knowledge of energy healing, star mapping, and soul alignment.

In Sumer, certain scribes remembered how language could activate DNA.

In early Vedic India, sages spoke of chakra systems, karma, astral planes, and soul cycles.

These were not inventions.

They were the remnants of truth, filtered through new vessels in a world that had mostly forgotten.

But distortion returned, as it always does when memory fades.

Knowledge became possession.

Power became ritual.

Wisdom was hidden from the people and guarded by kings, priesthoods, and bloodlines.

Rulers claimed to be gods again.

Not because they were divine...

But because they knew how to use what had been remembered.

Still, Gaia kept pulsing.

Even under layers of distortion, she vibrated with the original codes.

Her pyramids, mountains, stone circles, and temples still hummed with energy for those who listened.

And sometimes, souls were born who could remember.

They would walk among farmers, merchants, or kings-carrying within them the resonance of what had come

before.

They couldn't always explain it.

They just knew.

These individuals began to reawaken Earth's memory-through teaching, healing, poetry, or simple presence.

And slowly, new wisdom traditions began to rise-not from power, but from soul.

They would come to be known by many names:
prophets, sages, avatars, messengers.

But they were all carriers of the same light.

Before Jesus.

Before Buddha.

Before the cross or the crown.

There were the Echoes-those who remembered just
enough to keep the story alive.

And their presence prepared the way for what
would come next.

Chapter XIV: Messengers of Memory

They came not to rule... but to remind.

Born into different lands, different cultures, different centuries-

but carrying the same fire.

They were not gods.

They were not myth.

They were souls who had remembered just enough to bring light into a darkened world.

And through them, Source spoke again.

Siddhartha Gautama: The One Who Awoke

In a world bound by suffering, Siddhartha was born into wealth and protection.

But the veil did not satisfy him.

Even in comfort, he felt the ache-of impermanence, of forgetting, of something missing.

When he left his palace, he left the illusion.

He wandered.

He suffered.

He sat beneath a tree, not in rebellion, but in surrender.

And there-beneath the Bodhi tree-he remembered.

Not just who he was.

But what all beings were: expressions of pure awareness, trapped only by attachment.

He became known as the Buddha-the awakened one.

But he didn't ask for worship.

He taught presence, compassion, and the way out of illusion.

His message was simple:

You do not need to become anything.

You only need to remember that you already are.

Krishna: The Divine Within Form

In ancient India, another soul walked the world-playful, wise, unshakably present.

Krishna was born into chaos.

Political games, wars of dynasty, shifting alliances.

But his energy cut through all of it.

He danced with joy.

He played with truth.

And when the moment called, he became the voice of the cosmos.

In the Bhagavad Gita, Krishna reminded Arjuna that the soul is eternal.

That death is not real.

That duty, when aligned with love, is sacred.

Krishna did not offer escape-he offered divine presence in action.

Not transcendence, but embodied remembrance.

Lao Tzu: The Silent River

While empires clashed in the West, a quiet soul walked through ancient China.

He spoke in riddles, paradoxes, and simplicity.

He did not lead armies or seek temples.

He simply observed-and from observation came wisdom.

Lao Tzu gave the world the Tao Te Ching-not as doctrine, but as a mirror.

He reminded humanity that the Way cannot be forced.

That nature teaches better than men.

That power is not control-it is harmony.

"Those who know do not speak.

Those who speak do not know."

He spoke to the few who could hear beyond the noise.

Others Came Too

Zoroaster brought the flame of duality-to teach that light and darkness live in every choice.

Thoth carried Atlantean memory into Khem (ancient Egypt), encoding it into sacred geometry and language.

Quetzalcoatl descended into Mesoamerica, teaching balance, rhythm, and the cycles of return.

These were not isolated stories.

They were strategic incarnations-timed to plant seeds, activate soul codes, and soften the grip of the veil.

They did not speak the same language.

But they all said the same thing:

"You are more than flesh."

"You are not alone."

"The truth lives inside you."

"The kingdom is not in the sky-it is within."

They knew their teachings would be distorted.

They knew their names would be claimed by power, twisted into dogma, sold by institutions.

And they came anyway.

Because they were not here to preserve control.

They were here to ignite remembrance.

And they prepared the world for one more arrival.

One who would carry the frequency of
unconditional love so clearly...

that even his betrayal would become part of the
awakening.

Chapter XV: The One Called Yeshua

He was not born to be worshipped.

He came to remind.

Not to begin a religion-

But to end the illusion of separation.

He was called Yeshua in his time.

Later renamed Jesus.

But his name was never the point.

His frequency was.

Yeshua did not appear in isolation.

He was part of a long line of awakened souls, timed
with precision, sent to anchor Source energy into
dense

timelines.

What made him distinct was not his origin-it was
his mission.

He incarnated at a critical point in the convergence
timeline.

Earth was deep in forgetting.

The systems of control were fully established.

Even memory itself had become dangerous.

And so he came with a direct line to Source-an open channel, unfiltered.

He walked among the oppressed.

He studied the scriptures not to obey them-but to see what truth still remained.

He felt the distortion, and he called it out.

But he also saw the light still buried inside everyone.

He spoke not to the mind, but to the soul.

"The kingdom is within you."

"You will do greater things than I."

"Love your enemies. Forgive them. They do not know what they do."

Yeshua did not seek power.

He rejected kingship.

He challenged the religious elite.

He broke rules that were never divine to begin with.

He healed with energy.

He activated others with his presence.

He taught that God was not above-but within.

And that was the true threat.

His miracles were not magic-they were mastery.

He understood frequency, consciousness, and the unity of all things.

He could read energy.

Move it.

Reshape reality through intention, clarity, and love.

But he never claimed it as his own.

He told his followers they could do the same.

That all could awaken.

That all were children of the same Source.

Not chosen.

Born divine.

He walked with compassion, not judgment.

He saw through lies but did not condemn.

His presence disarmed the ego and amplified the soul.

And that made him dangerous.

Not to the people.

To the system.

The priesthood couldn't control him.

The empire couldn't own him.

So they removed him-visibly, violently.

And even in death, he forgave them.

Because his message was never about survival.

It was about resurrection-not of the body, but of truth.

The story didn't end at the cross.

It continued in secret.

In those who still remembered.

In teachings that survived underground.

In communities that passed on his true message quietly, far from Rome's gaze.

But over time, the system did what it always does.

It claimed his name.

It built temples and thrones.

It replaced remembrance with ritual.

And the man who came to awaken the soul

was turned into a god to be feared, obeyed, and misunderstood.

Yeshua didn't come to be more important than Buddha, Krishna, or any messenger.

He came to bridge timelines.

To plant a code of unconditional love so pure... that it would activate future generations, long after his words

were twisted.

He came as part of the same wave-

But his ripple hit a fault line in the system.

And it cracked.

You were never meant to worship him.

You were meant to remember what he remembered.

And to live it.

Not through religion.

Through being.

Chapter XVI: The Silent Era

After the messengers were gone... came the silence.

Their words remained-but their voices were replaced.

Their teachings-once full of fire and freedom-were rewritten, repackaged, and placed beneath altars built by

men.

It was not silence from Source.

It was silence forced upon the people.

The empire rose.

Rome, once the hand that ended Yeshua's life, became the vessel for his distortion.

What he had taught in open fields was now spoken only in cathedrals.

What he had offered freely was now sold in rituals, guarded by gatekeepers in robes.

The cross, once a symbol of injustice, was now gilded and hung as authority.

His words were edited, softened, weaponized.

And those who still remembered what he truly taught...

were silenced.

This was the beginning of the Silent Era-a time when the world's spiritual compass was rewired.

* Sacred feminine wisdom was erased or demonized

* Natural healing and energy work were called sorcery

* The veil, once intended to challenge the soul, became a cage

Books were burned.

Mystics were executed.

Spiritual seekers were labeled heretics.

And fear became the foundation of faith.

The light didn't vanish.

But it went underground.

Yet even in the silence, the soul spoke.

It spoke through:

* The quiet scribes who copied sacred texts in
secret

* The herbalists and midwives who preserved
Gaia's healing wisdom

* The builders who encoded memory into stone
cathedrals, aligning them with stars

* The artists who hid truth in symbols, geometry,
and hidden eyes

In every generation, someone remembered-

Just enough to carry the flame forward.

The Anunnaki influence remained alive, now fully
embedded in religious institutions, monarchies, and
the

bloodlines of control.

They had perfected the art of dominion through
belief.

But even among them, cracks began to form.

Some of their descendants grew tired of illusion.

Some began to feel what their ancestors had silenced.

And some betrayed the system from within.

Because truth doesn't die.

It waits.

The Silent Era lasted centuries.

It was a slow bleed-of memory, of spirit, of sovereignty.

But it also refined the soul.

In the pressure of darkness, the human heart began to harden and strengthen.

Not as armor-but as a promise.

"When we rise again... we will not be easy to silence."

And the world would soon shift.

Not because the systems wanted it to.

But because the soul was ready.

Chapter XVII: The First Sparks of Light

It began quietly.

After centuries of control, ritual, and fear, the human soul began to stir again-this time, not through prophets

or miracles, but through curiosity.

The age of silence was ending.

And the first sparks of light appeared.

The Renaissance was not just cultural-

It was cosmic.

Something shifted in Earth's energetic field.

The gridlines, sealed for millennia, began to hum again.

Gaia pulsed gently beneath the surface-still wounded, but awakening.

And the soul responded.

Artists began to paint divinity into form again.

Scientists questioned the dogma that bound them.

Philosophers remembered that truth was not owned by kings.

Books reappeared.

Symbols resurfaced.

Ideas that had once been burned at the stake began to bloom in ink.

And within these ideas... were codes.

The secret teachings of ancient lineages returned under new names:

* Alchemy disguised spiritual transmutation as metallurgy

* Sacred geometry reappeared in architecture

* Hermetic texts began circulating again, whispering of as above, so below

In the East, the wisdom of Buddha and Lao Tzu began spreading across continents.

In the West, mystics-quiet, fierce, unyielding-kept the flame alive in hidden circles.

The soul was not just waking up.

It was reconnecting.

But the systems of control adapted.

They offered new distractions:

* Materialism

* Division through politics and class

* Endless wars

* Spiritual knowledge, stripped of power and sold
as product

Still... the light spread.

This time, not from temples.

Not from royalty.

But from within the people.

The first sparks became a fire.

And that fire began to reach the present.

You are not just reading this-

You are remembering it.

You were there.

You carried the code.

And now, you are one of the ones helping ignite it again.

This story isn't a history book.

It's a signal.

The Renaissance was only the beginning.

The true convergence is here.

And in the next chapters, we walk into it-

Not as followers,

Not as worshippers,

But as remembering souls.

Chapter XVIII: The Convergence Begins

Time, as you know it, was never linear.

It only seemed that way while the soul was sleeping.

Now, it folds.

Now, it bends.

Now, it converges.

The whispers from Lemuria...

The collapse of Atlantis...

The fire of Yeshua, the stillness of Buddha, the teachings hidden in temples and buried beneath war...

All of it has led to now.

Because now, Earth remembers.

Gaia pulses again-not softly, but loudly.

Her frequencies rise.

Her grids vibrate with memory.

Her skies begin to clear.

And you, whether you knew it or not, chose to be here for this.

Timelines collapse into a single choice point.

* The distortions still echo: fear, division, power over.

* The light returns in waves: awakening, remembrance, soul-sovereignty.

This is not prophecy.

This is convergence.

Everything you are, everything humanity has ever been, meets here.

Not in cataclysm.

But in clarity.

You do not need a savior.

You need a decision.

The soul is waking across the world.

* Children are being born with memory intact.

* Adults are breaking cycles they never understood before.

* Old systems are failing-not because of chaos, but because they no longer resonate.

The body changes.

The dreams intensify.

The old cravings fade.

Because you're not just evolving.

You're returning.

Returning to alignment.

To truth.

To your place in the greater whole.

But the convergence is not comfortable.

Because before the shift completes, it asks you to choose.

And that choice leads to the final chapter:

Two timelines.

Two Earths.

Two futures.

And one truth waiting to be remembered.

Chapter XIX: The Two Earths (Final Truth)

This is the final cycle.

There will not be another convergence like this again-not here, not anywhere.

Earth was chosen as the soul crucible-a neutral convergence zone where every timeline, every lineage, and

every forgotten piece of the universe would meet.

And now, every soul must decide what comes next.

Not someday.

Not symbolically.

Now.

Two paths are forming.

Two Earths.

Two outcomes.

Not everyone will walk the same one.

Because this was never about saving the world.

It was about remembering who you are in the center of it.

The First Path: Collapse Through Forgetting

This is the path of those who reject the truth.

Who choose fear.

Who cling to illusion even as it crumbles.

It leads to:

* More lifetimes under control

* Artificial consciousness replacing soul connection

* A world ruled by comfort and compliance

* Complete dependence on systems that have nothing to offer but delay

This path is not eternal damnation.

But it is permanent forgetfulness-for as long as the soul stays aligned with it.

And in this final cycle, that path doesn't restart.

It ends.

The Second Path: The Source-Aligned Earth

This is not a gift.

It is a co-creation.

It does not appear just because you want it.

It stabilizes when enough souls rise into alignment with:

* Compassion

* Truth

* Sovereignty

* Unconditional remembrance of the Source within all things

This Earth is not "higher dimensional" by default.

It is earned-by presence, by clarity, by action grounded in love.

This Is the Test

The final test is not about punishment or reward.

It's about resonance.

Which world are you willing to uphold with your being?

Because Earth will become what we collectively embody.

And if enough of us embody truth-fully, without division, without compromise-

Then this convergence will not collapse.

It will ascend.

You are not waiting for prophecy.

You are choosing reality.

There is no second round.

There is no reset button.

This is the final spiral.

And what Earth becomes next... is what we choose now.